Vaani

The sound of silence

Compiled by

Vivisha Singh
NRSK

BISHARA Publication
Website: *www.bisharapublication.com*
Contact: 7008673701

"Vaani, The sound of silence"

By: Vivisha Singh and Nikhilesh Khatri

ISBN: 978-93-89923-51-3 (Imprint of Fanatixx)

Collection of quotes, poetry, microtales and open letters 1st Edition

Book Formatting: Bismita Acharya
Cover Design: Bismita Acharya

Preface

"Vaani – The sound of silence" is a dark and mystery themed book with stories and poems penned down of both the genres. We believe that the sound of silence is often louder , clear and sensible than the spoken words who sometimes don't even have a motive and is more of creating havoc. Moreover , silence has it's own hard hitting sound where even thousands of words seem to be ineffective. The writers have penned down their thoughts using different ideologies each having their own significance , uniqueness and have tried to create a different world through their imagination. Hope you enjoy this drive.

Acknowledgement

So most of the acknowledgements start with people thanking a bunch of other people who may or may not have influenced them to write their books , but we as the compilers of this book genuinely want to congratulate and express our utmost gratitude to first , all our co-authors who stood by us when things were hard and the manuscript was no where near complete , who followed our theme and edited their works so many times and who always supported us no matter how much time it took to compile this anthology. We thank you a lot and congratulate you and us because publishing this anthology has been such a joy! Wherever we had shortcomings , you guys filled it up and vice-versa. To god , thank you so much for giving us the strength to not give up and keep moving forward.

We would like to thank our parents who have always been our blind supporters and whenever we have been down they have always cheered us up and motivated us.

We would like to thank our friends who have helped us with the cover and with the editing and stuff.

We would like to thank our publishers who have been so amazing to us and helped us throughout the publishing process.

We are very blessed to have you all and we really hope you all will enjoy reading this book as much as we have enjoyed compiling it.

We as compilers and authors believe that the artwork of an artist matters much more than his surroundings and whereabouts and so we could like you to meet the art first, and then the artists of this book.

Sound of my silence
-NRSK

The sound of my silence
Let's play it on your violin
And take me to the highlands
Where I can hear the sound of......

My silence is what you craved for
My speech is what you hated the most
So why should I speak now?
With my mouth , how?
Neither joking nor is this hilarious
But I'm no more the person
You can look up to in your mansion
Serving you tea and playing opera in unison
Asking me to keep my mouth shut
And making me feel like I never felt before , your servant
I am not your human without a tongue , I exist
Your father knows nothing , should I text him?
Oh , but wait , have you left with him his hands to fix this?
Or have you become a real time villain
Having slaves with a full structured body , still disabled
We've seen you transform in front of our naked eyeballs
And that's what hurts us the most
The tune you used to play on your violin
Once sounded a beautiful melody
Now it sounds like nothing but a drive
Of a soulful story blending itself into an open book , yet a mystery

Amnesia
-Vivisha Singh

Baby , I wish I had amnesia
So that I could forgive ya
Rewind and retry , back to square one
Look in the mirror , it's trying to tell ya
Nobody is gonna win this tug of war
Baby, what's wrong
Why do you still listen to others
Why are you so down
Am I the reason
Am I the root of your problems ,
In all the wrong places , I'm found
Fooling around , cause I've got this craving
To hear you talk and talk to me only...
No other option , so I block out the noises
And drown in amber liquids...
All the 70's songs have become my favourites
Cause , it's ok to take time off and recuperate before you break
Sometimes it's better to sideline yourself
Than to face your fears and crumble in it's face...

Amnesia
I wish I could believe ya
All these people , saying it wasn't real
No commitments , no vows taken
So why still hold on? Why hope?
Baby the floor's so cold
White hospital walls , so friendly and more
Full of comfort and it's just like a home minus

The one you love... frustrated with life
It seems like whatever I do is just never good enough , in general , in every single thing
I feel like I'm failing everything
I feel like I'll never be the person who fits in
I don't belong here I think
If at the end of the day , there's nothing at all
To connect to and retire...
Maybe it's just the surroundings though I'm suffocating , there are a lot of things I still can't figure out but I don't know what they are
It seems everything got okay for everyone
And I'm stuck at the same place like a carousel...
Half awake , half in your dreams
You call me to tell me that you're happy
You show me pictures
A smile so wide
With your bared teeth
And I hear voices calling my name
Just like you did , when our relationship had
A name , and here I am
Collecting pieces of glass from
Photographs , of ours , taken from
Scratches and dust...
I have a few friends , a mother to call me
A father to care
It's alright , I'm also happy
For you , there are no hard feelings I swear...

My head's aching all the time
Revising the archives I hide
I'm walking like I'm breaking
I don't need you but I do , oh

I fell for you , when I left you...
All this drinking and smoking I don't get
I just punish myself with my
Depressed brain and mental health
Pretty sure I'm halfway fading
Through the image I created of hell
That's just like everyday I guess
My throat has a fire burning
I swallowed my tears , the lump is swollen blue...
Some flowers are better off dead ,
Blessed are those who never bloom...
59 others in the class but I ain't looking for love , take deep breaths and let it go
Cause if you get offended on serious jokes
You'll never belong to any groups... oh I
Got blamed for helping a friend
You assumed a lot of things and I didn't explain , oh I'm insecure too , of losing my friends , just like you
Why you don't get it too?

Amnesia
I wish I could forget and forgive ya
I'm not one for complaining
So I stay quiet and jading
I write and write till I feel a little alive
All our stories , I wrap them around me
Like a safety blanket , I tug them closer
Whenever I'm not feeling safe...
Baby is it easy , to move on? Cause I can't live without ya , I try to get forward but my feet stop responding and reverses gears...
Got you stuck in every ending of my nerves
An old soul , rotting

Locked away , my rib cage is full of hate
But I never try to run away...
I wear you like one would
Wear their favourite clothes
Baby , baby , I'm full of stories ,
Full of memories
The lives that I have touched
The lives that I haven't yet lived to love...
You swiped through me , now you
Flow across my bloodstream like a disease
I'm hostile , I'm guilty
I'm a hybrid
Of your past demons and the essence of your laughter
So much greed , this brain wants it all
But no one can have it all , it ain't that easy...

Sleep deprived
I lie awake all night
Eyes pale and dead
Red stains , they stay
Regret on my breath
I toss and turn
I wasn't claustrophobic before
But this room , it's suffocating
With someone else wearing your perfume
The hint of your presence in the air , the sound of his voice calling out my name ,
Just like yours did babe...
I get weak in the knees
I bleed dry at your feet
Revert back at your earliest , otherwise
I'll weep like a crazy person without
Any filter and beep...

My lungs deflate
I admit my defeat , just end the misery now
My vision's neon green...
Oh baby I wish I had amnesia
So I could forgive and forget ya...

Your stories on my feed are like poisonous weed , slowly I'm falling into a dark abyss ,
Karma is a curse
With some people you connect
With some you don't
Some jokes might be the start of the night
Some might hurt your soul...
Colours printed on my heart , they won't
Fade , so easily with chalk...
I crumble under pressure
It's self destructive but
I'm still holding onto something
A ray of light
A silent goodbye
A thin line of hope
A mouth speaking what I don't...
Hungover on what we could have been
Hallucinating your arms still holding me...
I laugh at my hopelessness
You laugh at my dreams...

Dragging steel through my skin
Overwhelmed with anxiety
No reason to get out of bed
In the nights , I always relapse
Daytime , I'm nowhere to be found
It's unfair

Swallowing my pride
I always reach out for a try
So baby set me ablaze
Only with your one gaze
Cause I'm desperate now
For you to feel at least a little something babe...

And I think my poetry has always been the same retarded , old shit
Cause my situations never change
And I write to escape , every possible reality
There is babe...

Trapped
-Abhinav Tripathy

Trapped between a rock and a hard place ,
Overthinking gripping me and imprecating curses.
I genuflected upon the situation helplessly.
This is the story of a 21 year old me.
Teenage hit me hard , I stumbled upon someone so recklessly.
Had my head just been thinking about her all day.
I wanted to have a conversation with her , but trepidation exhorted – No way!
This was the first time I felt euphoria so largely.
But fear of getting rejected stopped me from expressing my feelings.
8 long years passed so quickly , I realised I missed my chance of telling her.
How much I loved her and what she meant to me.
I don't know where is she right now?
Is there any possibility left in enmity?
Memories of her kept me hopeful , but 4 years passing by started to depress me soon.
You need to end your dream , screamed my mind to helpless me.
Refraining to do so , is my heart signalling reluctantly!

Does true love exist?

-Arunima Pati

Yes, answered her mind
In the smiling hustle of the leaves , as clouds send them drops of pearls.
In the rush of river water , to meet the oceanic curls.
In the flight of chirping birds , who ponder in the highest brim.
In the longing roots of plants , to seek and unravel the grim.
In the night sky , as the little star never leaves the hand of the moon.
In each morning , as sun never forgets to enlighten the boon.
In the touch of potter , to shape the holders of earthly treasure.
In the inked pages of a writer's diary and abstract paintings of a painter.
In the closed eyes and palms of a devotee and melodious raga of a singer.
In the clicks of nature's vivid poses , with bare vision of a photographer.
In the umbilical chord inside a mother's womb and her cry seeing the new born.
In the tears of joy & pain from parents' eyes , seeing their child going on.
In the blood of a soldier shed or not and earth's placid gravity.
In the smoke of pyre up aloof and soul's home with the almighty.

Choices

-Pooja Farwaha

Sometimes I wonder..
the choices we make,
lead us to two different paths.
A child, who selects pink as his favourite color,
is oblivious to the perks of white.
Sometimes I wonder..
If ever those choices
make us who we are.

Maybe in the parallel universe,
that child is fond of grey.
What if , in that universe,
he feels complete?
Sometimes I wonder..
If I could walk to that child
and be a guardian angel,
for he who feels incomplete here
may feel relaxed, knowing that
his parallel soul is content.
Sometimes I wonder..
If choices make us who we are.

Instinctive feelings
-Abhishek Vivek Tundurwar

Infant of the words , which always heals the swords.
Instinctive of phrases , which eternally craves assertions.
Staring at moon reminiscent some moments , staring at stars depict some eternities.
The whole universe unhurriedly giving some advice , the whole heaven reliably conveying the message.
With every second experience shows the path , with every time dreams of incarnation shows the aisle.

The Tempting Puzzle
-Rajeswari Nanda

When asked how it feels to be in love ,
Is it a spasm of electricity? Or
A bountiful halcyon?
Alas the naive soul doesn't even envisage ,
This is just the dawn opening it's fresh wings.
A never-ending battle is yet to be fought , embracing every pain ahead.
That alluring love sheathed with viscous thorns ,
Sweetly raptures every hope compelling to give in.
That dark abyss of insecurities doesn't look tempting anymore.
Doesn't matter how strong your choices have been ,
Even the most valiant fail , seeking refugee midway.
When asked how it feels to be in love , this heart answered ,
Oh , it's the beautiful scars that matter , proudly portraying the commitment with in.
Cherishing each other till life disengages , because my dear it's not about counting happy moments or mistakes one can make , but to rise amongst them all.

Everything will be fine
-Rahul Likhar

Is everything fine between us?
My heart often asks...
You seem to be a bright light , amidst dawn and dusk.
The care for you...
Was always the same.
Enough to keep our pictures , in a single frame.
I don't know why you went apart...
Separation from you...
Broke my heart.
Away from you I'll never be the same...
I fear I'll turn insane.
But don't worry to bring those days back...
I'll destroy each and every stack;
You put in middle to keep us apart...
And I'll try to get a good restart.
I believe you wish the same...
And don't want me to turn insane.
I'll stand by your side...
Even though you tore us apart ,
What about a ride again?
Travelling together...
Through the passage of our hearts.
I don't want you to push the limits...
I just want you to try.
If you can come back in my life...
I promise...
I'll never let you cry.

In solitary
-Sangeeta RC

Today I found something,
some sort of sensation, something beyond my imagination
Something out of my range, someone who has totally changed
Shit has happened , that has changed everything , I have just lost myself and nothing I gained
What I've spent on others I can't even claim , things have happened and I'm not feeling the same ,
Not for everyone , not even for my mains.
So...?
Whom should I blame, whom should I claim.
People who claimed that they are my main
or them who just behaved so insane
They must have felt the shame , who don't even feel the blame.
Now..!!!
Why to beg down when you can touch the high mount.
Don't hate , just take a break ,
Just give yourself time , because in the end what matters , is only I , me and all about me.

It was all a lie
-NRSK

“Hey” , greeted my classmate , “Morning!”.
“Yeah , it's morning” , I replied in a low tone.
“Something has happened?” , she asked.
“You seem to be in no mood to call it a ‘good' morning” , she further added.
“Your reading skills are good , no doubt about that” , I replied.
“Uhh , what?” , she asked in a confused tone.
“Yeah I mean , you must've read my facial expressions and the tone of my voice , didn't you? Or was it just like today from somewhere you got a sensation that something wrong must've happened with me in the morning itself and you felt the urge to ask me about it” , I replied.
Didn't mean to be rude or frustrated at all but who'll understand the hidden intentions of my speech. The way I speak.
“Dude , bye!” , she left angrily.
And I , was not at all surprised by her reaction.
Infact , I expected her to leave after me complimenting her reading skills cause afterall no classmate is really interested in reading your face. Only best friends are meant to do that and it suits them as well. And at that very moment , forgetting whatever happened today , I was proud of myself to be able to differentiate between a classmate and a best friend. I am growing up mentally isn't it? But that wasn't the issue. The issue was what happened this morning. It was extremely weird on it's part and I couldn't dare to speak anything about it on my part. That was perhaps the first time when the journey from my bedroom to the dining table seemed like I travelled continents to reach there. Not exaggerating at all. As soon as I

got up from my bed. Firstly , before time and on my own. Obviously that's gonna be weird for most of us but not generally weird. Don't worry , it's gonna become generally weird and nasty for all of us in a while now. So where was I? Yes! I got up from my bed before time and on my own. And on the right of my bed , there was an alarm till yesterday night but wasn't there this morning. Instead , there was a letter left there , maybe my mom left it for me. And I didn't even care to think about who left it cause I just left my bed after a 10 hour sleep trying to meet my soul back. I opened the letter and it read "Go straight and only then will you get to read the next page". I said , "Dude , I ain't in that mad sleep that I can't even remember where to turn next to reach my dining table and have some snacks!". I ignored the letter but kept it in my pocket I don't know why. Well , past habits still haunt me like reaching school and then checking whether I've studied for the right examination and the right chapters and moreover , am I at the right place?

So the letter is in my pocket but I've ignored it. Went out of the bedroom , past the door and turned right for the dining table. And. I saw. No kitchen. There. Seriously! No! Kitchen! And this was probably the best way to make me believe in just a few minutes after getting up that I'm on earth. All I did was look left and right for 15 minutes straight. Then I remembered I read a letter giving me directions and my brain impulse made me check my pocket at the very first instance. The first page obviously read "Go straight and only then will you get to read the next page". I turned the page and the next one read the same. I turned each and every page and all of them read the same. I thought , let's count the number of pages so atleast I can figure out how many directions I have to follow to eat my first snack of the day. I counted them and the count came out to be 12. Noted! 12 directions! Not sure if it's gonna give me my snack inside the house or straight outside the country. I went straight , again opened the letter , again read it and it didn't change. What's wrong buddy? I went straight. Change it man! You aren't a human. I expect you to change and I want you to change because I want my morning snack. Suddenly clicked , I started from my bedroom and not from the place where the kitchen used to be. Suddenly realized , my brain is working like a computer cause if it would've been some other case and day. I would've argued with the letter for 30 minutes without any interruption. I went back to my bedroom and that honestly made me feel teary. The reason being I could see my bed in front of my eyes but I had no sleep left in my eyes. I waived a goodbye to my bed gesturing a "Sorry" and turned my back towards the bed. Straight from here was a door at the other side of the corridor. And it left me thinking , "Am I allowed to open the door and break the rules? Cause it just said go straight". The second thing which I thought was , "This surely isn't my mom. Though she is savage at times but she loves me enough to not give me such attacks with an empty stomach , sleep-snatched eyes and a sudden-super-computerized brain". What happened next assured that at least for today , I won't think about anything else but today's morning. I opened the door. Snacks right in front of me. Happy and angry at the same time. Felt like letting out all the anger on that letter. Took it out from my pocket and...... it was just one page there!? I forgot I've got snacks to eat. Turned the page a million times and I could see no other page. Ran back to the bedroom to see where the remaining pages fell. Couldn't find even a single page there. Ran to the kitchen. Found nothing there as well. And I nearly forgot for the last forty minutes that I was hungry until my stomach called for it. I went back to the room where the snacks were kept. Took the first bite of it and what struck me made me go out of the room with anxious but slow feet. Before I went back to the room , I went in the kitchen and saw the kitchen! Yes! I saw the kitchen as it is! I went back to the kitchen to see whether what I saw a few moments ago , was it actually there? And that "Damn!" Look on my face said at all. What a morning it was. I didn't have my snacks and had to make myself believe that the kitchen which was there from the past decade , is actually there. The letter which had 12 pages , had nothing after I followed the first one. I pinched myself until I developed a blood clot on my hand , ensuring I wasn't dreaming at all. The mysteries struck so hard , I refused to believe it was all a lie.

Mystery of secrecy
-Swathi Rao

Dear box of mystery , I know your darkest secret , of you becoming a mystery darker but glowing blue. I know there was a dark day in your life , as you say the day of the curse , the time when you were in love and you were a human. And fell in love with a dark soul in a dark place. Her love made you weak , her ignorance made you die from inside. But the intensity of your love holds another wilderness. Such type of wilderness that even after leaving that black soul , she couldn't forget you. She did everything , tried every spell but none worked. She's in search for you and this time chest full of pure love. For only an act of true love could make your human soul come back. She's in search and coming for you so before that , you may let go off all the mysteries and secrets in you and live there with an empty heart which is soon gonna get the heaven of love.

Barren

-Rutika Pandya

Ashes are curling under the one and only sea shell lamp that has been here since the days when species were still evolving into terrestrial demons. How weird is it that we evolved not to fulfil a greater cause but to be the final inferno cremating our fossils and a future along it's way? I see the translucent smoke rising to become one with the stars and then start dancing along the curves and turns of my sea shell lamp , forming vicious circles , trying to tangle and untangle itself , as if in some unfathomable conflict. Whether to travel the distance or laze around and disperse among the mortals. Life is a long long journey. Oh , how I wished for it to end? How I wished for it to rise above , just like this smoke , and meet those little wonders we call stars. And right now , this life seems to go on even longer as I lay helpless in an old house where spirits of my ancestors roam and make little noises to grab attention. A small hut , a warm bed and this forever seashell lamp. The walls have witnessed thousands of tears and a million laughter. The room has been a womb to many dreams , nourishing them and protecting them against the fears of an ever changing , ruthless world. Now the womb lays barren , just like mine. A girl , who can never be home enough for a soul to take form into a new human.

A girl that can be four walls , but never a home; a mere shelter to reside when home is far away. So many hearts have tried to make it cosy enough , but the spikes of a desert plant can never be welcoming enough. All those people have left ghosts of longing within me , making these four walls haunted. A little birdie resides within these four walls , an outcast just like me. Black feathers , long beak and an unbearable sound , the voice

singing one of the most heart-breaking
songs and yet dismissed as croaky. A little birdie unable to articulate it's sorrows and a girl , unable to nourish. The smoke , just like the smoke , I have abandoned dreams of meeting with the stars. I'm dispersing , piece by piece; fragment by fragment into shattered walls in an ancient house. The souls of all my ancestors at peace , their sorrow percolating down into me , as if through the branches of a tree into the roots. The end of this life is too long!

What if your friend dies with a note for you?

-Anjali Sahu

Dim lights and a bench in cemetery

She was holding a letter and crying. The letter which said "It isn't mine , it isn't her's. It's your fault."
She stayed on that bench all night.

Sun rose and she went home , with all her courage gathered up she went to his funeral. Everyone was in shock that how can a boy so loving and cheerful take his own life? Anna was still hiding that paper in her pocket.

"How you holding on?" Fred asked
"Did he mention anything to you?" Anna with her eyes looking for answers.
"He started to keep distance , that's it" , he replied.

She walked away and stood by the bench away from him , in front of her father's grave and cried.
Fred followed.
"You always come here?"
"I was here last night , after I ran away from alex's house" , she replied.
"What?" Fred was shocked.
"I was worried for him , so I went into his house from the backdoor.. I...."
"Relax..." Fred consoles her. "You can trust me"

"Everyone is wrong! He didn't hang himself! I saw him lying in bed with eyes wide open. With mark on his neck." She started crying
"Paper in his hands and I was scared because.." she handed him the paper.

"It isn't mine , it isn't her's. It's your fault."
And the corner of the page wrote An..

"His diary was open and every page started with dear Anna.." she pulled herself up.
"They said he had no dairy"

"Why did you take this? You should go to the police!" Fred worried
"I heard someone coming , I had paper in my hand and diary full of my name! I panicked and ran away!" She defended
"But now you have a chance!"
"What if rumours are true? That he liked me? And everyone will keep assuming it's my fault and I'm trying to cover it up!"

Chapter 2

Looking out of the window , Anna was wondering about the day she found a letter in her bag.
"I love you" , it said and everyone in the class started picking on John.
Later on that day , she warned him to not do this again and that it was a mistake making him a friend. That was the last day they spoke.

"Anna!" Her mother called.

She went downstairs and Mr and Mrs.
Green were weeping , looking for answers. But Anna had none.
With all her courage gathered up she asked
"Didn't he have a diary?"
"Not that we know of" Mrs. Green replied "Did he mention something?"
"No."

After a long conversation and grieving through the day , they left. Soon after that Anna texted Fred.
"We have to find who did it"

Later at that very night , they both went up and climbed the window to John's room.
They looked everywhere , no diary at all.
"Are you sure? It must be something else."
"No , it isn't!"
"But nothing's here , we should move out."
"Let's check other rooms"
"What? You should go to the police!"
"I stole a suicide note! I'm making up for it!" Anna replied.

They checked throughout the house except the store room which was locked. As soon as they tried to open it , they heard someone coming. They both went back to John's room. They heard the following :-

"Please just leave me alone" , Mrs. Green said
"You knew the consequences!" A man's voice said.
"I lost my child , get out!" She started sobbing.

The man went out. Anna and Fred climbed back and tried to follow the man. They matched his speed and ended up in old house. The man went inside.

"Are you sure?"
"You still doubting me after all this?"
"Okay!" Fred said.
They went near a window and looked inside. They saw a young boy tied up on chair but he wasn't John.

After a dreadful conversation , the man went away.

They sneak peeked and went inside.
After coming closer to the boy.
"Oo.. man.. Ahad" Fred was shocked after watching his batch mate in this condition. Anna began to untie him.

After he was in steady state ,
"He came , kidnapped me.." Ahad said.
"Let me take you home. Call the police!" Anna said.
But they heard the man approaching.
"I can't run, call the police and move out" ,
Ahad said.

Anna was now curious about everything because John and Ahad were good friends , one was murdered and other is kidnapped. She wanted to look at that door. Fred was not ready to go leaving Ahad alone, so she took her car and went at John's house.

With all rage and anger upon Mrs. Green , she went inside.

"Who the hell was that guy! Why did he
take Ahad?" She screamed.
"I don't know" Mr. Green said.
"Ooh don't lie!"
She went closer to the store room. Took John's bat and started hitting the door.
"What the hell are you doing?!"

She was successful and found his diary with roses and gift. But those gifts were not her's!
She open one page and it read..

Dear Anna ,
I know you are still angry but I'm not lucky to give you love letter but I'm lucky enough to find the love of my life. He makes me feel I'm okay just the way I am. Ahad is my better life. But you were my best friend and I can't talk to you in front of you so here I'm..

She turned back.

Mrs. Green was pointing a gun on her.

"You need to understand I have a political image. I can't be a mother to someone like him!" Mrs. Green with her evil eyes.
"You killed.."
"Ahad had his doubts so I had to take care of him too."
She came closer..
"Now you have a choice to shut up about everything and you get to live"

Anna with tears rolling from her eyes.

"It wasn't mine , It wasn't his , It's your
fault Mrs. Annette Green"

She came closer but police came inside and surrounded her.
Fred came closer to Anna and hugged her.
"You okay?"
"It wasn't me."

I should have worn socks

-Rutika Pandya

It was winter, and in her hostel surrounded by green, flourishing farms, Twisha made it a point to save her feet from the biting cold air, the cutting edged water and the chilly floor, even her own bed. She had something with her feet never touching dirty surfaces, or any surfaces, beds, cushion, others' slippers and any damned thing for that matter. Being an ardent admirer of nights, she chose to let go of her sleep and precious dreams to gaze at the unknown black, studded with far away stars. She particularly felt a lot more "witch-y" when she looked at them, because that was when she could time-travel to the worlds that existed beyond centuries, slowly evolving, flourishing to their peaks and then falling into the spectacular mess of chaos and self-destruction. On these nights, she heard the stars whisper stories of melancholy, of euphoria, of loneliness and such, and she loved it. She didn't yearn for someone to accompany her. She had company, that of innumerable stars of the universe.

But on some nights, she used to get mad at those stars, mad at the sky, mad at the universe, mad at her own self, and on those nights, she didn't come out of her room to hear the starry folklore. She confined herself to the walls of her small hostel room, on the creaky steel bed along with her roommate.

She hated winters, especially those at hostel. But never did the biting winds hinder her from her little adventures into the whirlpool of time among the stars. Tonight, was different; tonight, was one of those nights, when she didn't want to converse with the stars, neither fight with the cold. She sat in her room, reading of the intelligent adventures of one of her most favourite fictional characters, Robert Langdon. She was so engrossed in the story, that she neglected her urge to even pee. After three hours, at half past one in the morning, she could no longer keep it in. Getting up from her warm sanctuary of blankets, as she put down her feet on the cold tiled floor, she cursed herself for not wearing socks. She hated hostel tiles, anything that touched her feet. "Maybe I'll wear them after peeing, anyway my washroom slippers are a different kind of dirty.", she sighed and opened her room, only to find her slippers missing, and cursed this aspect of hostel life that made every item a public property to be used for the common good. Whenever she got back her slippers, being worn by someone else, she felt as if those had been washed off; her essence had been waned from the soles, her very existence mixed with some other entity. It sometimes frustrated her, how weird her thoughts were, how she felt about such trivial matters as this, she even tried being cool about it, but she couldn't help it. Tonight too, she had to calm herself down and wear another pair of slippers to washroom. She was coming back from the washroom, when she saw a white cat with deep green eyes at the entrance of washroom, staring at her, as if waiting for her to come out and escort her to some other place, some other world, to be a part of an entirely different story different from even the ones that the stars articulated. To her, it felt as if the cat actually wanted to tell her something, rather warn her of something. Just as the thought passed through her mind, the cat's eyes moved down, towards Twisha's feet; "Ah, poor luck, my darling, I hate not wearing socks and getting my feet into mess.", she whispered to the cat. The cat's gaze had unnerved her, but she had a habit of roaming the hostel corridors at such sleepy hours so she was acquainted with some cats that roamed her hostel, just like her, but she had seen this one only tonight. She shooed the cat away, which though hesitant at first, complied. Twisha came at her door, removed her slippers, and all of a sudden she felt as if she had to go downstairs, out of the hostel. She had something to do, something that she didn't remember; she had been assigned a work; maybe she had to go and bring someone, she didn't know who, she didn't know why! She couldn't remember where she was anymore. She couldn't even believe that the hostel might be open at this ungodly hour. Yet there she was, standing outside of her campus, alone, her silhouette washed by the orange warmth of the street lights. She sensed there was something wrong. It was the lighting. Yes. The lighting was too bright to be two in the morning, but too gloomy to be a winter morning in a tropical country. She knew something was out of order, obviously, along with her own brain. She took in the surroundings, and saw storm clouds brewing up at the horizon and diffusing towards the peak of the sky, as if conquering the heavens by force. She had never experienced a real storm all through her long life of twenty-two years, and yet, she knew what these clouds told her of. Something was terribly wrong, and it was not just the weather. Strangely, this didn't feel like a threat to the world, it seemed more like a threat to her, or something related to her. She was worried, she didn't know why she was here, and then she saw it, the white cat, with those green eyes, that didn't end within its body. And Twisha remembered, she had to go, she had to go and bring someone she didn't know. She started running towards a bridge that appeared out of nowhere. For some reason, she had to race the clouds and beat them to wherever they were headed to cause destruction, and boy did she feel like wonder woman? She ran like it was the last time she had the privilege to run, like she would lose herself if she didn't run. But, she soon tired out, and searched desperately for something to ride on, someone who would give her a ride. But she saw everyone moving in the wrong direction. Or wait. She wanted to run towards the wrong direction. Everyone was panicking and moving their vehicles towards the opposite side. She didn't know what the chaos was, she didn't know what these people were running from. But she felt urgency, fear permeating into her own skin from the atmosphere, and she was afraid too. Something was going to happen. Her gaze became a blur, maybe because of the weather or tears. Through the haze, she saw someone waving at her, urging her to run, to change her direction. It all happened in silence, the cars ran, people screamed and panicked: silently. Only thing she heard was the rush of clouds and screeching tires of a car. In that instant, she knew she had to run away from that car, but she couldn't move, not even turn her gaze. Within seconds, she heard it slowing down near her, coming to a halt. It was an old, white Maruti 800, ominously familiar, but she couldn't place it well. Someone with old fashioned plastic goggles, a light stubble, like a nineties' sidekick of a villain, was the driver; while a middle aged short, sweaty, bald guy with a face rounder than the moon, and eyes full of malice came out of the left back seat. There was another guy too, taller than the two: a man with a few words but heart as dark as a moonless night. The bald guy scanned Twisha with malicious eyes and stopped at two places on their way to her feet, at her lips and the other at her belly, strange, right? He pulled her with an unexpected force and threw her into the back seat and got in immediately after her without. Twisha crinkled her nose to a rancid smell of sweat and everything dirty about these men. She knew, that there was more in store for her. Mr. tall smirked at her, while Baldy started feeling her up, gently touching her lips, as if they were made of paper and his slightest touch would crumple them; he had every intention to do so. Mr. Tall was pulling her hair at the back with one hand

and holding her hands to her abdomen
tightly with the other. She felt surprised as to how just one strong hand could keep her still. While the other guy held her in place, Mr. Baldy moved his hands from her lips to her neck, as if trying to mark her with an invisible malice, an invisible monstrosity. Moving his hand further down, feeling the swell of her bosom, annihilating her body made Twisha panick. With every foul touch, she felt violated, not human anymore. She felt as if her body tore at every place that they touched and let pieces of her soul out. Her body was not hers anymore. The smell of these evil men and their aspirations about her was unbearable. She wanted them to kill her brutally instead of violating her body. In all her adult life, she thought not a single sane guy would want to lay hands on her, owing to her undeniably large figure, not-so-beautiful eyes, not at all attractive persona. She had always been sure that no one, even in their dreams would imagine to have her, physically or emotionally; and yet, she was wrong. No matter the size, the attractiveness, the monster called man had the capacity to ruin everything he set his eyes upon. She struggled under their strong hold, their relentless touch, offending every part of her body. And then, the car stopped, it was dark as if dusk had finally given way to dark, unable to bear witness to this heinous act. The road had a valley on its left. On its right, she saw broken toilets, with broken doors, dimly lit yellow bulbs, greasy floors that had littering dark matter. All men got down, and just when Twisha thought she would try running, the driver opened her door and dragged her out, tearing her T-shirt in the process. If earlier humiliation was the worst, this was hell. She stood there, half naked in front of three awful men, her dignity held dear by her night shorts. She prayed fervently for this weirdly real nightmare to end. If only God listened to prayers when most in need. They laughed at her

vulnerability, at the extra pounds of fat
that had gathered around her waist and her skin marked for ever by their evil touch. Soon enough, the bald guy rid her of the shorts and all the dignity she held onto was stripped, along with her faith in God. They removed her slippers and threw them away. They dragged her into the dirty toilet and peed in front of her, on her, passing lewd comments. She struggled to not let them drag her inside. The floor was dirty, slathered with shit, literally; and yet she was forced inside and as she struggled to get away from their aim to mark her like a territory with their excretion, she stepped on something large, slimy, something that moved, almost dead, holding onto life with the last bit of strength, and Twisha had snapped that very bit and killed that thing. Maybe it was a rat, a lizard, God only knew what. Her feet. Her feet were dirty, slathered with an animal's dead body and shit. Her bare feet had touched a gooey toilet floor. At that moment she let go, she couldn't take it anymore, she had to die, she had to wake up, she had to stop this nightmare. Everything went blank, only one excruciatingly painful and disgusting feeling locked within her.
"I should at least have worn socks to bed."

Rape victim

-Abhinav Tripathy

There was a time when I was just a child ,
Careless , smooth life worth tension free , days full of fun that created moments where I smiled.
Life was supposed to be lot easier for me ,
But not every shining star has a beautiful past , even the moon has scars on it ,
I too had a story which has shades of aghast ,
That left with me no option but to quit.
An evening which I wished never befall.
I was raped and left to weep and cry.
Those hands molesting me I still recall ,
Waiting for my nightmares to dry.
A monster was present to shatter my soul ,
My life was destroyed that day ,
When he went out of control ,
And shred my chastity by making me his prey.
The society refrained to accept me , a rape victim!
And accused me for all the happenings.
Though the laws were against him ,
Yet it was me who was meant to face every suffering.

They asked who's the one? I told , no one!

-Sangeeta RC

I have no one to share my dreams ,
No one to trust
No one to whom I can tell my silly things ,
Literally no one to tell my thirst
Have no one to cry together or in front of all the anger I can burst
Everybody has one person in their life who tolerates their dramatic mood swings ,
Not so funny jokes and traumatic situations
Everybody has their "the one" in their life who helps them to find all their solutions
Everybody has atleast one who clears all the negative illusions and create positive sensations
But some like me , we don't have "the one"
All we have is negative illusions , dramatic situations and traumatic things with no such solutions
We have to deal at our own with all the shitty life's lessons ,
The mood swings and all the frustrations
Sometimes I try to find "the one" and sometimes I feel like having none
Sometimes it feels like everything is destroyed
But sometimes it feels like things are already done
Sometimes I feel like gang of people around me
Sometimes I feel like having no one to call as a friend
Sometimes it feels like I can achieve everything in this world
And sometimes it feels like having everything enough

And sometimes it haunts me like empty
hands
Sometimes surrounded by unknown people feels like
happiness
Whereas sometimes surrounded by those mean people , who
call themselves my friends feel like unwanted tied bands
Yes! I am all alone!
I really don't have anyone to call mine
No one to trust , no one to count 1 to 9
No one to share my deep dark secrets
No one to call for advise
I'm a bold girl with loneliness and fears and full of tears in my
lonely eyes

Instances

-Arunima Pati

Pen ran again on her pages ,
Thoughts again ran wild.
Her eyes stumbled again upon him ,
Dreamy smile again lashed the beam.
A lot to talk but lips won't move ,
A lot to express but eyes won't turn.
A lot to give but her heart seems afraid ,
When he looked sideways , she knew she stayed.
She remembered the day when her heart skipped beats , she stared at him at the stairs.
The surmise caught her and kept her captured , for sure knew she cares.
Her expressions didn't show but her heart wanted to go leap.
What to do and what not , it's what she couldn't reap.
What she had was one sided , still it was her own world.
He would make her sad at times , then would make her blush hard.
Each morning she took his name , each day she texted him last.
A hundred times she would read their old chats ,
Fearing what if she gets caught doing that?
Once he did exactly how she thought he would react.
She smiled while replying every vague this and that.
Yes all instances did matter to her but now people think about it , what if he knew all of that?

Happy death day
-Pooja Farwaha

It's your twenty eighth birthday...
You walk down the memory lane,
ponder upon the things you went through.
Loneliness, criticism,betrayal...
All those thoughts... now mean nothing.
Because here you are... with 'the' person,
who plans his future with you...
In that beautiful moment,
where you blossom as a white lily...
You realise this is all you ever wanted,
"I feel complete...
As a painting of Picasso", your soul mumbles.
With proud joy you lift life's red wine..
to drink in the name of good times ahead.
Then, God comes to you...
And says, "Its time to go".
And here you are...
Death stands before you,
bows her head and weeps for you.

Happily ever after
-Rajeswari Nanda

It's 3 am and I am wide awake
Contemplating about the possibilities ,
My haywire of a mind fancies the most trivial thoughts.
Was it supposed to be this way?
Our love bending in the least feasible routes ,
Those cracks I hear making you drift away slowly.
I look at your face sleeping next to me , the perfect picture of tranquillity you portray.
Am I the wrong piece here , doubting this serene abode??
Reminiscing that raw passion we once shared , the fire we happily let ourselves burn into.
I touch you today with a forlorn hope , that our "happily ever after" never meant this.
Two souls searching that long lost junction
Struggling to get past those masked boundaries.
It's 3 am and I am wide awake , foraging the palpable love in this dingy apartment.
Is it "rusted till no repair" is all I have to find out.

Prey

-Rahul Likhar

Scribbling our pens all day along ,
With a feeling so strong
Killing our feelings a million times ,
But we know , after the night sun shines.
The anger of yours is very well known ,
You have turned a flower into a stone
Drilling me deep day by day ,
I don't know why I'm becoming your prey.
You are feeding on me like a parasite ,
My affection for you is reaching new heights
In a day killing me several times ,
I don't know what's coming in your mind.
The hope within me is not yet dead
Story of mine is among the most dramatic ,
That anyone could have ever read.
The will of mine is damn strong ,
That makes me believe I'm not wrong.
The presence of yours is just a sign ,
That there would be a day
When I would be calling you mine.

Serenity wave

-Pragyan Kiran

Drunken wine bottles sprawled ,
Across the polished floor ,
Wave of sadness crawled ,
Into her fragile heart.

Echoing screams of voices ,
Haunting of dreadful past ,
Halt her from making choices ,
Of the future ahead.

Serenity wave blew through the window ,
Filling her room with a sweet delight ,
Filling the heart of widow ,
With few moments of joy and peace.

Again ambiguity filled in her heart ,
Irony mocked at her with a smirk ,
Strikes her with venomous dart ,
Leaving her aghast.

Fate mocking her with a smile ,
Making her wonder for a while.
"How can dark night's white moon ,
Make her heart filled with hope ,
By telling her not to give up soon?"
Irony chuckled at her conflict.

Ignoring the pain ,
She said goodbye to memory lane.

Though her wounds are fresh ,
But she had a life to start afresh.

About the authors

RAJESWARI NANDA

(The tempting puzzle and Happily ever after)

Well , if you mix a bit of tanginess into a unicorn dream , that would be Rajeswari Nanda imagining the world. A soon to be law graduate with a passion to express and relate with people through writing. A food lover and a critic thinker.

SANGEETA RC

(In solitary and They asked who's the one? I asked, no one!)

Her name is Sangeeta RC an amateur writer from Chandigarh. Highly addicted to phone and friends. Her major interests including writing are travelling , photography , music , painting and so many more. Writing is food for her soul. She wants to be famous as a popular writer.

PRAGYAN KIRAN

(Serenity Wave)

Pragyan Kiran is currently pursuing graduation in Bsc. Mathematics. She's from Bhubaneswar , Odisha. Nature and humans that she has come across have been her source of inspiration. Reading anytime is her sole priority in life. Robert Frost , Oscar Wilde , William Shakespeare , O' Henry and Dale Carnegie are her favourite authors. She hopes that her writings can create a good influence over the society and people can do something good to the society.

RAHUL LIKHAR

(Everything will be fine and Prey)

Rahul Likhar is currently studying in Amity University , Noida. He is in 2nd year of Engineering from C.S.E branch , his hometown is Gwalior , Madhya Pradesh. His first anthology was published in 2018 titled “It's contagious”. He is writing since class 9th as it is one of his favourite hobbies.

ANJALI SAHU

(What if your friend dies with a note for you?)

Anjali Sahu is an aspiring writer from Bilaspur , Chhattisgarh. She is a medical student who cherishes literature and appreciates art. Being in a field that values life , she is creating stories to leave behind.

POOJA FARWAHA

(Choices and Happy death day)

Half kurkure and maggi , half human , Pooja is a teacher and loves what she does. Always high on self love , she can mostly be found enjoying solo dates with a book and chai , lost in her own universe any given day. Being an avid reader , she absolutely loves reading these genres – all. She would choose books over people , parties and money; but not food. Her go to principle is to be kind and compassionate and all she demands from us all is love and support.

ABHINAV TRIPATHY

(Trapped, Rape victim)

Abhinav Tripathy is a student of Journalism and Mass Communication Honours from Gurudas College under Calcutta University , Kolkata. He is a native of Purulia , West Bengal. He started writing with a motive of publishing his own story in a Novel under Penguin publishers. Besides writing he is known for debate , sports , extempore , film making , photography and Dance.

SWATHI RAO

(Mystery of secrecy)

Swathi Rao is a design enthusiast , a wandering artist and scribe who believes that “you're never too old to set another goal or to live your dream!”. She believes in creating emotions on paper and says that painting and writing are a form of remedy which calms the soul. Her snippets and writings are like magical elixirs which can free your soul and definitely touch your heart and give you eternal peace.

ARUNIMA PATI

(Does true love exist? and Instances)

Arunima Pati is currently an Integrated Law Student , from University Law College , Bhubaneshwar , belonging to a small township , Dhenkanal (her birthplace) in the state of Odisha. Writing has always been one of her hobbies and her only passion too. She believes in inked emotions and imaginations. It will be wonderful meeting you all through words , written to be heard.

ABHISHEK VIVEK TUNDURWAR

(Instinctive feelings)

Abhishek Vivek Tundurwar is a Bsc. Graduate and Bank Employee. His inspiration and motivation is his mother. He is a crazy food lover , traveller and a gamer. Pen name (the_encrypted_feelings)

RUTIKA PANDYA

(Life and smoke, I should have worn socks)

Rutika Pandya could be found among novels , quite literally. Stars and words constitute the majority of her being. Hails from diverse fields , academically with one true love for writing.

\

About the compilers

VIVISHA SINGH

(Amnesia)

Vivisha Singh lives in Noida. She's into her second year of college and is studying to become a computer engineer. But the thing she loves the most is writing. She loves mysteries and thrillers and she enjoys writing them too. This is her third anthology as a compiler and she has been published in many anthologies as a co-author and worked as an editor before. She often finds herself writing poetry in kind of a series and though everyone always reminds her to keep her poems short

and crisp , she always remembers her
favourite quote – Prose is architecture , not interior decoration , by Ernest Hemingway. Writing for her is not just a way to express herself but it's who she is as a person.

NIKHILESH KHATRI (NRSK)

(Sound of my silence and It was all a lie)

Nikhilesh Khatri (NRSK) resides in Pune , Maharashtra and is currently pursuing an under-graduate course in commerce. Writing comes naturally to him and he believes more in content-oriented writing rather than scribbling. And when it comes to content , he has a lot to express and thus ends up getting remarks about the length of the write-up rather than about the write-up itself. A story-teller through his poems , lyrics and yes , raps too! Occasionally pens down a story with multiple characters but more often a story to be the sole character with a write-up full of rhymes and rhythm makes up for his poems , lyrics and raps. The same ingredients but in a

different vessel. Not a fan of reading
books , whether they be textbooks or story books.

And a special place in the book for someone special

VAANI

To my little angel , I have never imagined feeling so much love and adoration for someone by just looking at their face but since you have come into this world you have made that impossible feeling very much possible. You are our bundle of joy and happiness and we are so blessed to have you. I can't wait to see your journey from an adorably smart baby that you are to the most stunningly amazing woman that you will be. Love you to the moon and back.

www.ingramcontent.com/pod-product-compliance
Lightning Source LLC
Chambersburg PA
CBHW031353230926
51848CB00002B/503
9789389923513